Samuel Orzabal and the Strange Discovery

Story and artwork
by

Paul Wills

Copyediting: Rachel Mann

For my family for their encouragement
For Darryl S. Bill C. and Frazier H. for keeping me motivated!

Contents

Part I

Chapter One   The Call   Page 1
Chapter Two   Finders Keepers   Page 11
Chapter Three   Recovery   Page 17
Chapter Four   A Saucer Full of Secrets   Page 22
Chapter Five   Revelation   Page 28
Chapter Six   Giants   Page 36
Chapter Seven   Bugged Out   Page 43
Chapter Eight   Home Grown   Page 50

Part II

Chapter Nine   Revisiting   Page 58
Chapter Ten   Fellow Prisoners   Page 64
Chapter Eleven   The Incident   Page 73
Chapter Twelve   I, Spy   Page 82
Chapter Thirteen Energy Crisis   Page 90
Chapter Fourteen Home Again   Page 97

PART I

Chapter One

The Call

This was one of those days – rain, cold, wind. You name it, the elements were throwing it at us. It was the perfect day to hide away in the basement, tinkering with the old radio device. This was Sam's father's CB equipment and you practically had to be a scientist to operate it. There were plenty of dials and buttons and levers everywhere. There was also a large microphone attached to it.

Sam had first-hand lessons working with it, courtesy of his dad. He knew almost every function and loved to impress his friends with his ability to find interesting conversations – as well as listening for aliens from space!

Sam's companion today was his cousin, Jamie. She

was the same age as Sam – in fact, their birthdays were only one day apart (Sam was the older). Jamie was the same height as Sam, and had brown eyes and collar-length wavy red hair. She was an unabashed tomboy who got along very well with Sam.

It was a holiday week, so Jamie was spending it at Sam's house.

"Listen. Usually around this frequency, I can make out some weird voices," said Sam, as he turned a giant knob on the device.

"What kind of voices?" asked Jamie.

"I don't know," replied Sam, "just some faint, weird voices."

A crackling of static was emanating from the lone speaker, but nothing out of the ordinary.

"I think you're hearing things..." started Jamie.

"Shhh. Listen."

Sure enough, there was a kind of garbled noise coming out of the speaker. A few more turns of the dial and it was almost audible.

"...*need assistance...*"

"Hey – it kind of sounded like they said, 'need assistance'," Jamie pointed out.

"...*shpl plais ...*"

They listened a bit closer.

"...*sam...*"

Sam pulled back and stared at the receiver.

"Did you hear that?" he said.

"I did. It sounded like he said your name, but of course, that was just a coincidence..." Jamie said.

"Yeah, I know but still pretty weird," said Sam.

Further listening revealed nothing more than static,

so the novelty of the experience quickly wore off. Sam shut down all the equipment. The silence now highlighted the blustery conditions outside.

Sam and his cousin climbed the stairs into the warmth of the living room, where Sam's mom already had the fireplace burning. She was extra hospitable when there was a house guest.

"How about some hot cocoa to warm you both up?" she offered.

"Sure Mom, thanks," said Sam.

"Thanks, Aunt Sue," said Jamie.

"Marshmallows in mine!" Sam added.

"Coming right up," said Mrs. Orzabal.

Sam's mom was a throwback to another time – she loved to wear polka dot dresses, her jet black hair styled from the 1950's. She had soft eyes and her bright red lipstick showcased her warm smile.

Sam turned to Jamie.

"Too bad it had to rain today. We could be outside exploring the woods behind the house."

One of Sam and Jamie's favorite pastimes was hunting and digging for potential buried treasure. Even if that treasure was an old bottle – the discovery of any object was a lot of fun.

"Guess what I found out? There was a meteor crash near here a long time ago. My dad was telling me about it yesterday," said Jamie.

"Really? How nearby? That would be something cool to investigate. Where did it happen?" said Sam.

"I don't know. All he told me was that it was kind of a big deal back then. It was in all of the local newspapers for a while, but nothing ever came of it."

"Wow! What if it's still there?" said Sam.

Talk of the mysterious meteor crash continued until Sam's mom returned, holding a tray with two steaming cups of hot chocolate. Sam and Jamie appreciatively took their cups and savored the intoxicating aroma before slowly sipping the hot chocolate.

"I put your marshmallows on the side, dear, in case you wanted some as well," Mrs. Orzabal said to Jamie.

"Thanks very much. It's delicious," said Jamie.

"Mom – did you ever hear the story about a meteor crash nearby?" asked Sam.

"Oh, yes. But that was quite a while ago. Your grandfather would tell me stories about that day. He was here when it happened."

"Mom! How come you never told me about that? You know I live for that stuff!" said Sam.

"Well, to be honest, it's been so long that I forgot," said Sam's mom.

"Where did it crash?" asked Sam.

"Somewhere far into the backwoods. Only a small group of neighbors went off looking for it. But because it happened in the thick brush of trees, nothing was ever found."

"What about the authorities?"

"They didn't make much of it. The newspapers eventually wrote it off as folklore," said Mrs. Orzabal. "But you know what?" Sam's mom said, with a sudden change of voice. "Gramps said it was an alien ship."

Sam and Jamie felt a twinge of excitement.

"Why would he think that?" asked Sam.

"Well, for one thing, he said he saw it."

Sam turned to face one of the corners of the house.

There was a very comfortable-looking recliner occupying that area.

"Is that true, Gramps?" Sam asked.

"Of course it's true! You know I never tells no lies," came the response.

Grampa Bucky was ninety years old. His favorite pastime was sitting in his comfortable chair with his favorite dog, Penny, resting on his lap. (Peaches, their newest dog, was a little jealous of this.) His second favorite pastime was sleeping. It was always great when he could combine the two. He would occasionally wake up to make comments or pointed observations – sometimes it was in reaction to what he had been dreaming about. All in all, Gramps was in pretty good health for his age.

How did you happen to see it?" asked Sam.

"Well, it was late in the evening and I had just finished choppin' some firewood. I heard a loud screeching noise and looked up to see a silver object hurtlin' toward the ground!"

"But Gramps, that sounds like it could have been a meteor," said Sam.

"No, it wasn't a meteor. This thing was round and silver."

He continued, "There was a loud crash – scared me half to death! and soon after, I saw smoke over the trees. I thought about going to investigate but it was too close to dinner time. I did go out the next day, but I didn't see nothin'. Some newspaper people came around asking questions and I told them what I saw but they ended up writing it off as just a meteor crash."

"Wow. Now I *have* to check out the crash site," said

Sam.

"Oh no," said Sam's mom, "You already know I don't want you going deep into the woods, Sam. You know how easy it is to get lost in there."

"I know, Mom – I won't, don't worry." said Sam.

But the seed was already planted in Sam's head. One way or another, he was going to find out more about the mysterious object that fell down to Earth all those years ago.

*

After dinner, Sam and Jaime turned their discussion back to the crash.

"...You know we should go see for ourselves," said Sam.

"Yeah, that's just too crazy of a story to pass up," said Jamie, "Let's do some investigating of our own tomorrow."

"That's what I was going to suggest," said Sam.

"What about your mom?" Jamie reminded him. "She said not to go out looking for it."

"Well, she said 'don't get lost in the woods'. We'll just make sure that we don't," Sam answered.

The more they talked about it, the more excited they became. They talked about the possibility of what they might find until it started to get late. Jamie was staying with the Orzabals for a few days, so it was convenient for them to make plans and carry them out – but now, it was time for bed.

"Goodnight, Sam. See you in the morning," said Jamie.

"Not if I see you first! Ha ha!" said Sam. Jamie rolled her eyes.

Sam brushed his teeth and changed into his pajamas. By the time he crawled into bed, he was already half asleep. That night, he had the weirdest dream...

He was riding his bike on another planet. It was a bizarre but beautiful world. Daylight had a very mellow blue-green hue. There were lots of trees, but they were nothing like the trees he knew. These were much shorter, the leaves blue and purple in color. They looked like something right out of a Dr. Seuss book. The dirt was not brown but an orangey yellow. It was a very vivid, wonderful setting.

As Sam was taking in the strange but appealing scenery, he came across a metal disc, half buried in the ground. It had plumes of smoke wafting from it. Sam ditched his bike and slowly approached the metal object. He touched it and immediately pulled his hand back. It was hot!

"...Sam...," someone faintly said, "...Sam, we need your assistance..."

Sam searched for the voice and eventually discovered that it was coming from behind the metal craft. He was shocked to find two small creatures – no taller than his thumb and wearing jet-black costumes that seemed to show the galaxy of stars twinkling within. The bodies were human-like, but their arms were longer and their elongated fingers seemed to point in every direction at once. Their heads were blocky with one large eye on one side and several holes (for breathing?) on the other. Only one being looked like it was still alive.

"Sam...please help us..." it said, but not with its mouth because it didn't have one. It spoke with its mind.

"...you are our only hope..."

Sam desperately wanted to help. He reached out a hand to lift the creature but before he could touch it, it vanished. The other creature vanished as well. In fact, everything around him started to vanish until...

Sam was awake in his bed.

Well that was the most bizarre dream I've ever had, he thought as he rubbed his eyes.

The alarm clock showed 2:15am.

I guess all of this alien spaceship talk is creeping into my dreams.

Wait a minute – that creature said, 'Sam I need your assistance'. Just like I heard on the radio. Is that just a coincidence?

Sam knew he wasn't going to fall back asleep anytime soon, so he got out of bed, slipped on his slippers and very quietly made his way back down into the basement. It was bitterly cold, but that didn't distract him.

He flipped on the lights and turned on the radio equipment. He knew the basement was soundproof to the rest of the house, so he didn't have to stifle any noises while he was down there.

Once the radio was back on, he slowly turned the large dial to the same frequency that he had heard the voices earlier. There was only static. Sam kept listening.

Static.

"Hey, what are you doing?!"

Sam jumped out of his skin.

Jamie couldn't help but laugh.

"You did that on purpose!" Sam said.

"Maybe," she chuckled, "but what *are* you doing down here in the middle of the night?"

"I had a strange dream and couldn't sleep. It was about that ship crash," said Sam, "I felt like aliens were trying to communicate with me."

Jamie gave him a look.

"I know – it does sound crazy but it felt real," said Sam.

"...*Samuel*..." the receiver crackled.

This time they both jumped.

"Ok – I know you heard that!" said Sam.

"I did. *That* was weird," said Jamie.

Sam and Jamie were now transfixed on the old receiver, waiting to hear what it would say next.

They didn't have long to wait.

"...*Samuel Orzabal...need your assistance*..."

The voice was a bit clearer this time, which didn't make it seem less eerie. It was a strange voice; almost electronic-sounding and with an unusual dialect. It would be an understatement to say that it rattled Sam.

Sam picked up the microphone and pressed the 'talk' button.

"Hello. This is Sam Orzabal. Who are you?"

"*Sam...we need your help...the ship...*"

"Hello? Hello? What ship?" said Sam, urging the voice to go on. But there was nothing more.

"This has got to be a joke," said Jamie, "but he *did* say 'the ship'."

"What if Gramps was right and it was a spaceship he saw? And maybe the aliens are trying to contact us?" Sam felt a little stupid for saying these words out loud.

"I think it's true," replied Jamie, to Sam's surprise.

"You do?" asked Sam.

"Yes. Your grandpa tells some pretty wild stories but this one I believe. He sounds convinced enough. Plus, the thing with this radio is a little too much to ignore."

"That's what I'm thinking. That settles it – tomorrow morning we start our search for that crash site," said Sam.

"First, we've got to get some sleep. We'll get started early," said Jamie.

Jamie walked up the stairs and out of the basement while Sam turned off the radio and followed suit. Once back in bed, it wasn't that hard to fall asleep after all.

Chapter Two

Finders Keepers

Sam and Jamie were up bright and early the next day - although not as early as Sam's mom, who was already brewing coffee and making breakfast.

Sam and Jamie were too excited to eat, but Mrs. Orzabal insisted on eggs and toast. Gramps was already sitting at the dining-room table waiting for his breakfast, with Penny ever at his side.

After Sam and Jamie scarfed down their food, they walked over to Gramps and quietly talked to him about the spaceship that he had witnessed crash down to earth.

"Hey, Gramps – me and Jamie want to try and find that crash site you talked about yesterday," said Sam in hushed tones. He didn't want his mom to overhear.

"I wish I could come with you. I've been wantin' to find out about that for a long time," said Gramps.

"Can you point us in the right direction?" asked Jamie.

"Yep. But don't tell your mother," he said to Sam, "I don't want you to get me in trouble."

"Mum's the word," said Sam.

After breakfast, Gramps, Sam and Jamie walked out onto the front porch. It was still windy and cold but much more tolerable than the day before. At least the sun was out, and the clouds had now dispersed.

Gramps stood up tall (as tall as he was able) and peered out over the vast number of trees. He seemed to flash back to that day, channeling the exact moment of the incident.

"Right over there," he pointed.

The direction was pretty vague, but at least it was a start. They could see on Gramps' face that the memory was still vivid.

"Ok, we're going to check it out," said Sam.

"Just don't go getting lost. Your mom would have a fit," said Gramps.

"We'll be super careful. Come on, Jamie – let's go get our stuff."

Sam and Jamie retreated to the basement to scrounge some supplies. They considered the basement to be their headquarters/supply room/communications room. It was perfect for this investigation.

Sam grabbed a backpack and they filled it with supplies – a flashlight, two long rolls of kite string, a hunting knife, a small hatchet, and a small shovel. They still had a few more items to add once they were back upstairs. A quick dash into the kitchen brought the remainder of their supplies – apples, a banana and a couple of quickly made peanut butter and jelly sandwiches. Now they were ready.

They carefully walked out into the backyard, trying not to let Sam's mom see them, and snuck into the thick of the forest.

"Ok, no turning back now," said Sam, "we're committed."

"I'm not even thinking of going back!" said Jamie, "let's tie the string around this tree."

Sam and Jamie came up with a safe way of going deep within the forest without getting lost. They would unravel the kite string as they traveled inward – and when they ran out of string, they would head back.

Once the string was securely tied to the entrance tree, they started on their trek.

It was always exciting to explore the woods behind Sam's house. Sam had lots of unusual but fun adventures here through the years.

"If we come across an old shack, we *do not* go inside," Sam said as a reference to an earlier adventure.

"Huh?" said Jamie.

"Never mind."

Sam never told anyone about his more outlandish quests for fear they would think he was crazy – or worse, a liar.

The woods had that slightly sweet 'nature' smell which was intoxicating – a mix of pine, flowers and earth. To Sam, this was heaven.

Jamie was just as enamored by the call of the wild.

But mostly for her, it was the thrill of the hunt for something unusual to be discovered.

"What if we do find some kind of weird ship? I think I would freak!" she said.

"I forgot to bring my camera," said Sam, getting caught up in the excitement, "just in case."

Sam and Jamie continued deep into the woods – crunching through foliage, rocks and dead tree limbs. Jamie was in charge of releasing the kite string as they went along. Occasionally, they would stop to rest and talk about the possibility of coming into contact with alien life. It was a very far-fetched concept, but it kept up their excitement. It may not be a spaceship, but they knew that Gramps witnessed *something* crashing into the woods all those years ago. Even if they came away with nothing, the adventure was worth it.

They were now deep into the forest and close to using the second spool of string, so they decided to take a break and enjoy the food that they had brought with them. They found a nice open area and retrieved the peanut butter sandwiches while saving the fruit for later. After practically devouring the sandwiches (hunting in the forest is hungry work!), they were wishing they had brought along something to drink.

"Well," Sam said, "we might come across a stream – we can drink water then."

"Yeah, how did we not know peanut butter sandwiches would make us thirsty? It would be nice if we could come across a milk stream," said Jamie.

After they finished their meal, they gathered their stuff and resumed the hike once again. It was close to fifteen minutes before Jamie announced that they were near the end of their second spool of string.

"Great. We didn't even find a crash site," said Sam.

"Look!" Jamie pointed upwards to the trees ahead.

Sam saw that Jamie was pointing at a section of trees that were badly misshapen. They didn't appear to fit the form of the surrounding trees. The leaves in the middle were darker and more mutated. Also, they looked like they were pushed outward.

"Well, that certainly doesn't look natural. We may have found our first clue," said Sam. "C'mon, let's check it out."

Sam and Jamie went as far as they could with the string.

"We'll tie the end around this tree," said Jamie, "but we can't go too far away without losing our trail."

"It's not that far – we'll just memorize the path," said an excited Sam.

They burst off running – making a conscious effort to remember landmarks along the way. They fought through vines, broken branches, downed trees, but they finally reached an area that looked a lot like a crash site. It was obvious that something had hit the ground here – there was a barren, indented spot on the ground where nothing grew. The trees were growing away from this spot almost in a circle.

"Wow. I think we found it," said Jamie.

"Yeah – something crashed here all right!" replied Sam.

They walked down to the center of impact, searching for the object that caused it.

"Let's get the shovel and dig here," said Jamie, who was all too eager to find something significant.

They each took turns digging as much as they could with the small hand shovel.

After around thirty minutes, they were able to dig a good two feet – before getting too tired to go any further.

"I don't think we're getting anywhere with this small shovel," said Sam.

"Let's take a break for a little while and we'll try it again," suggested Jamie.

"Good idea. We still have the rest of our snacks to re-energize," said Sam.

So they grabbed the last of their food – an apple each, and a banana. Sam and Jamie were so hungry that it didn't take them long to finish.

"Even if we don't find anything, at least we have a story to tell Gramps," Sam said.

"True. But let's see if we can dig up an even better story," said Jamie.

They each took turns digging again until they were now down to about four feet. It appeared that they were wasting their time – until...

CLUNK!

"Hey!"

Sam hit something hard. And silver.

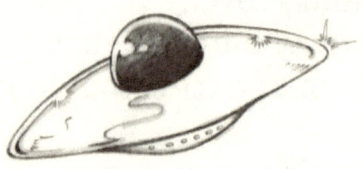

Chapter Three

Recovery

The object that Sam had revealed barely peeked out of the soil. It was smooth-polished and incredibly reflective. Sam and Jamie were beside themselves.

"Oh my God!" Jamie exclaimed, "We found it! We actually found it!"

But 'it' was still mostly submerged in the ground. They didn't know how large it would be, or if it was even possible to dig out, but they would give it all they got.

Frantically, they took turns digging around the object – when one was using the shovel, the other was scooping out dirt with their bare hands until the object revealed itself. It was a bonafide spaceship! But it was only three feet in diameter.

"Holy cow! This is insane," said Jamie.

They couldn't speak for a while – it was too much to take in.

The ship was small. It was made of a highly polished

silver metal and the top portion looked like deep black glass. The metal repelled the dirt – so you'd never know it had been buried for decades. There was no indication of an opening. The ship was surprisingly light as Sam pulled it out from its grave. "Can you believe this? I'm actually holding a tiny spaceship!" said Sam.

"Sam, we've got to get this back to your house. We can look it over once we get it back," said Jamie.

"I guess it's light enough for me to carry. Let's jet," said Sam.

With the alien craft in tow, they made their way back to where they had tied the kite string. The spaceship was cumbersome, but they managed. There was the occasional rest break for which they spent time staring at the ship.

"Sam, what about your radio in the basement? There's no way this is a coincidence, finding this thing," said Jamie.

"I know. I think we need to find whoever was contacting me and hope they can give us more info on what to do with this sucker."

Sam picked up the ship and they began their way back home with adrenaline keeping their pace brisk.

They finally made it back at the clearing of Sam's house, pausing once more.

"I think we need to keep this between us for now," said Sam, "I know my mom would freak out, and anyone else who found out would probably try and take it away."

"All right, I'll go ahead first and make sure the coast is clear. I'll give you the signal to follow," said Jamie.

Jamie casually walked across the yard, glancing back

and forth to make sure no one else was around. She reached the house and entered quietly. After a quick scan of the rooms, she found Gramps in his chair fast asleep. Mrs. Orzabal was nowhere around. Jamie made it back to the rear door and waved for Sam to enter. He picked up the ship and briskly walked into the house, going straight down into the basement. Jamie followed behind.

"We made it!" Sam exclaimed with a smile. He placed the ship on the workbench while he and Jamie pondered their next move.

They thoroughly searched the ship again but there was no indication of an opening. It was as solid as a rock. They tried to peer into the black glass dome but could see nothing.

"Let's try your CB radio," Jamie suggested.

Sam agreed and switched on the device, to reach out to whoever or whatever had been trying to contact him. He hadn't changed the frequency, so he just adjusted the volume knob. With microphone in hand, he spoke.

"Hello? This is Sam Orzabal, come in."

"Greetings, Sam," a voice responded. "Thank you for reaching out to us. We are in dire need of your help."

The voice was clear now. It was also otherworldly.

"Hello," said Sam nervously, "what help do you need from me? Who are you?"

"I am Shrad from the Seventh Star. We are some light years away from your planet. We have sent a searcher ship to retrieve what you know as 'gold'. It is necessary for our energy use. We were saddened to discover that our ship crashed in your location – we have been trying to make contact ever since. We had renewed hope when we received a signal from you and are confident that you can help us."

After a moment Sam spoke. "Wow. This is a lot to take in. We did find a ship."

"Yes, we know. We are very well connected to the ship. Unfortunately, two of our fellow beings were navigating the ship when it crashed. We believe they are alive but need to be revived."

This took Sam and Jamie by surprise – even though they were in possession of a spaceship and were now in contact with an alien being, it was a shock that they might come face to face with one.

"We can't figure out how to open it," said Sam, trying to come to terms with the situation.

"There is no opening in your traditional sense," said Shrad. "You have only to walk through the dome when it is necessary to enter. However, your current size prevents that from happening."

"Right. There's no way we could get in there," said Sam.

"This statement is not correct. There is a way to reduce both of you to the appropriate size, "said Shrad.

Sam and Jamie looked at each other again. Things were getting more surreal by the moment.

"How?" said Jamie.

"Place the ship in a stable position, rest your hands upon it and, when you are ready, I will remotely set in motion the transmorphing process."

Even though Sam and Jamie were excited, they were also quite scared of the prospect of shrinking in size and actually entering an alien ship.

After putting the ship on the ground next to the

radio transmitter, Sam gave the word that they were ready. A very strange sensation washed over them. The world around them was growing enormous! In actuality it was they who were shrinking at a rapid rate. Smaller and smaller until...

They stood on the plank of the now enormous spaceship. They had shrunk down to peanut size.

"Oh my God!" said Jamie, "I didn't think it would really work!"

"This is unreal. Look at the size of everything!" said Sam.

Indeed, every piece of equipment, furniture and tool towered over them. It appeared that if they fell off the ship, it would be like falling into the Grand Canyon.

"Ok, now that that's done, how do we get inside?" said Jamie.

Jamie reached her arm out to the glass dome and was surprised to see it pass right through.

"Sam, look!" said Jamie, whose arm was now halfway inside the ship.

"Looks like we found our entry," said Sam.

They each held their breath instinctively and took a step into the black dome. They were not prepared for what they saw next.

Chapter Four

A Saucer Full of Secrets

Gramps was wondering how the kids were doing. It had been a while since they went on the hunt for the crash site. He thought maybe they should be back by now. He picked up Penny from his lap and put her on the floor. She walked over to where Peaches was resting but Peaches stayed unmoved.

Gramps walked through the house and into the back yard. Mrs Orzabal was still out running errands. Gramps gazed in the direction of the crash but saw no sign of the kids. He figured he'd give them another hour and if they didn't show up, he would spill the beans to Sam's mom. He walked back inside and noticed that the basement door was open.

*

Sam and Jamie were awestruck by their new surroundings. They had managed to enter an alien space craft and their senses were overwhelmed.

Everything was smoothly polished and pleasing to the eye. The room was illuminated with no indication of a light source. There were multiple colors of light – some flashing, some steady. There were also multiple passageways, but Sam and Jamie had no idea of which one to take.

"Sam, we're inside a spaceship!" Jamie said, as if saying it would make it any more believable.

"Yeah, but what now?" said Sam.

As if on cue, the increasingly familiar voice of Shrad boomed through the ship.

"Welcome to the ship. Many thanks for your much-needed assistance. I will guide you to the area where you will find and help our fellow beings."

Sam and Jamie were starting to feel more at ease with their guide.

"We definitely need your help to find our way through here," said Jamie. "This ship is enormous! Hard to believe you were just carrying it around, Sam."

"This is definitely a solid '10' on the crazy meter, said Sam. "Shrad, where are the two aliens... er, beings?" He didn't know if using the term 'aliens' would draw offense.

"They are down the corridor and through a series of

doors, in the control room."

"And you think they are still alive?" asked Jamie.

"Yes, they are alive. However, the severe force of the crash put them in hibernation mode. They will be in stasis until someone can help awaken them. This is how our bodies deal with severe trauma. It takes quite a lot to remove life from us."

"How do we wake them up?" asked Sam.

"You will have to join their hands together, locate an ion phaser device and discharge it upon them," said Shrad, "That will bring them from their suspended slumber."

Sam and Jaime followed Shrad's instructions as he led them from room to room – each one radically different from the previous. Every room seemed to have a specific purpose – whether healing or experimentation. The current room was pure white and didn't appear to have any form. It played havoc with their senses and they had to follow directions closely to leave.

They eventually ended up in what was immediately obvious as the main control room of the ship. There were lots of monitoring devices, flight levers and too many buttons to count. There was also a disturbing sight – two lifeless alien beings sprawled out on the floor.

Jamie let out a gasp as they entered, and Sam stared in horror. These aliens looked remarkably similar to the ones in Sam's dream. It didn't appear that there was anything they could possibly do to bring these creatures back to life.

"We found them," said Sam, finding trouble to speak.

"Very good," replied Shrad, "I will give you instructions on how to revive them.

"Do we have to touch them?" asked Jamie, a bit grossed-out.

"Yes, you must join their hands. Once you do that, you must retrieve the regeneration device and use it on them."

Sam and Jamie slowly walked over to the unconscious beings and dragged them close together. They interlocked their hands as well as they could and stood back.

"Where's the device?" asked Jamie.

"Right here."

A holographic green arrow appeared off to the side of the room, pointing at something in the corner. When Sam made his way over, he saw that it was pointing at a laser gun resting within a glass compartment. Sam picked it up and walked over to the two aliens.

"Now, press the button on the side, point it at our colleagues and pull the trigger," said Shrad.

Sam did as Shrad said and felt and felt the gun vibrate. It made a strange high-pitched noise and then stopped.

At first, there was no reaction, but soon the aliens started to move.

"Whoa, they *are* alive!" said Jamie.

The aliens struggled at first but soon managed to sit upright and then stand. Sam and Jamie were mortified that they were standing directly in front of two unusual-looking aliens. They instinctively backed away, all the while keeping their eyes glued to these crazy looking creatures.

"Hello," said Sam, "We saved your lives!"

Sam wanted to let the aliens know that they were not enemies. The creatures seemed to be gathering their bearings before turning their attention to Sam and Jamie.

Greetings, humans. We are grateful for your assistance.

The aliens had no mouths to speak with, but Sam and Jaime could hear the words in their heads.

I am Serutuf and this is my companion, Erar.

Sam and Jamie felt a little more at ease and slowly approached them.

"My name is Sam, and this is my cousin, Jamie."

The aliens did some weird twirly thing with their arms and said in unison, *Hello Sam and Jamie.*

The aliens were friendly and grateful.

You have our deepest gratitude for rescuing us. We are an explorer ship on a mission to return a mineral from your planet, said Serutuf.

Erar continued, *Our ship was commandeered by a hostile entity. We tried to resist and that resulted in our ship crashing into your planet.*

"Hostile entity? Are they still onboard?" a worried Jamie asked.

No. It was a remote attack. He is well known in our galaxy for surprise attacks. We were not careful enough to avoid him, said Erar.

"Are they gone? Can the guide help you?" asked Sam.

What guide are you referring to? asked Serutuf.

"The boy is referring to me, Serutuf," said Shrad.

Serutuf and Erar froze at the sound of the voice.

Shrad., said Erar.

"Yes, it has been quite some time since we spoke. It

does me very good to see you are both alive and well. We have a lot of unfinished business."

"You already know him?" asked Jamie.

Yes. Shrad is the one who took control of our ship, said Serutuf.

Sam and Jamie suddenly felt numb.

Chapter Five

Revelation

"Wait a minute," said Sam, "are you saying our guide, Shrad, is your enemy?"

Yes. His race is notorious for hijacking ships and using them for their own purposes. Very similar to what humans would identify as 'pirates', Erar said.

"But he's the one who helped us get into your ship to revive you," said Jamie.

Yes, but it was only to advance his own means. You are pawns in his plan. I'm very sorry you were involved in this, said Serutuf.

"I find it very peculiar that an advanced race such as yours are still hindered by emotions," came a voice overhead, "Emotions only defy logic."

"Can you cut off his communication?" asked Sam.

Who was becoming quite disturbed by Shrad's voice.

"No, I am in complete control of the ship's communications," Shrad answered instead.

"What does he want?" asked Jamie.

He and his people covet the gold we set out to retrieve. He still needs for us to locate it and return it back to him. That is the only reason he cares for us to be alive. Unfortunately, he also seeks to bring humans back as a species of study – a male and a female, said Erar.

"No!" said Jamie, letting her fear take control.

"We have to get out of here. Can you please help us?" she said to the two alien beings.

I'm afraid we have no control over this matter. If we could help you, we would.

Just as these words were spoken, a door port opened off to the right.

"Now, humans, please proceed to the holding port until I give further instructions. Any resistance will be met with severe consequences," said Shrad.

Sam and Jamie had no choice but to do as he requested. They did not want to find out what 'severe consequences' would entail.

Upon entering the holding room, Sam and Jamie found it to be rather familiar. It had regular tables and chairs, pictures of nature, desk with lamp. It didn't look alien at all.

"What on Earth?" said Sam with no pun intended.

"Why does this room look like a normal Earth house room?"

"I think it's to make Earth 'specimens' feel less anxious. I saw an old television program that had this exact scenario," said Jamie.

"You are correct," said Shrad. "I trust you feel comfortable in this environment?"

"No. Far from it," said Sam, "We'd rather be in our real environment."

"In time you will get used to your new home. You are doing a yourselves a great honor – you are an important study for our race and a necessity," said Shrad. "Now, there is food available through the regenesis machine located within the wall of your room. Just speak whatever food you would like, and the machine will produce it for you. Please try to make yourselves comfortable. It will be some time before you are transferred to my ship."

Sam and Jamie were in no mood to eat or get comfortable. They were more focused on breaking out of there. They took a seat on the couch and spoke to each other in very low whispers.

"We have to come up with some plan to get out of here," said Jamie.

"I know. But even so, we're still super small...we also have to figure out how to get back to normal size. We need Serutuf and Erar's help but they seem to be just as helpless as we are," said Sam.

*

"Fellow beings, you must do as I say and maybe you can get back to your planet in peace," Shrad instructed the alien pair.

Shrad, we have little to no choice but to comply. What would be our mission? said Serutuf.

"It is very simple – find gold and bring it back to me.

I don't need much, since we can replicate it sufficiently."

Our ship is in the human's residence. We do not have enough power to transmorph through the walls, said Erar.

"Then you must use what power you have to manipulate the ship outside without the transmorphing effect. I can see you have enough energy available to fly through and out. I will help in any way I can. Please get started."

*

Gramps made his way down into the basement, carefully descending the stairs. The kids were nowhere to be found. He started to turn back before he noticed the metal spaceship sitting on the floor and dismissed it as another one of Sam's newfangled toys. He also noticed the transceiver radio equipment blinking.

"I keep telling Sam not to leave his electronic equipment on when he's not around," he said to himself.

He pressed the 'off' button and made his way back upstairs.

*

Erar and Serutuf immediately were aware that communication with Shrad was cut off. The communication signal indicated that all forms of contact were showing 'offline'.

Serutuf, it appears we are free from Shrad at the moment, said Erar.

Yes, we must make use of this opportunity and implement our chance for freedom, said Serutuf.

We will inform the humans and maybe they will aid in locating the gold, so we can return to our planet.

Sam and Jamie were not getting anywhere with ideas on how to escape. Their situation seemed quite dire and hopeless.

"What are Mom and Gramps going to think when we don't return?" said Sam.

"And my parents and sister. We're gonna disappear from their lives and never see them again!" Jamie started to cry. This made Sam feel very uncomfortable – he had never seen his cousin cry. Not even when she broke her arm in a baseball game. She was always the tough one. But then again, this predicament definitely justified a good cry.

"Don't worry, Jamie. We'll get out of here. We just have to put our heads together and think," said Sam.

Unexpectedly, a side door panel slid open. Sam and Jamie looked up to see Serutuf and Erar standing in the walkway.

Hello humans, said Erar. *We have need of your assistance.*

"Did Shrad send you?" asked Jamie.

No. In fact, that is why we are here – to defy him, said

Serutuf. *There has been a malfunction of some sort which caused his communication with us to disconnect. We do not know for how long, but we need to act quickly to permanently disconnect from him.*

"Yes! We'll help you if you can get us back to normal size," said Sam.

Yes, we will do that in time – but first, we need to replenish our ship with the gold's energy. Once we do that, we will restore your size and flee your planet, said Serutuf.

Sam and Jamie followed the aliens back into the control room, where they discussed what they would do next.

Our ship is extremely low on power. We suspect Shrad was getting signal assistance from some other source located near us and there was an interference or disruption of some sort, said Serutuf.

"Gramps!" said Sam.

"What?" said Jamie.

"Shrad was initially communicating with us through the CB radio. I'm thinking that Gramps probably came down into the basement, saw that I left the equipment on and turned it off."

"Yeah, he's always on you for leaving things on in the house," said Jamie. "In any case, he did us a great favor."

Indeed. Now we must fuel our ship if we are to return you to normal size and fly back to our own galaxy, said Erar.

We need to find pure gold. We must locate and retrieve it from your earth, said Serutuf. *Let's get started.*

Serutuf and Erar led them down the corridors until they reached the dome of the ship, where Sam and Jamie first entered. The aliens walked through first, followed by the cousins. The feeling of passing through a solid object was something Sam and Jamie were still not quite used to.

Once outside the ship, they were ready to begin their quest.

"Wait a minute – how much gold do you need? I think Gramps has some gold coins locked away in his desk," said Sam.

Then lead us to it, said Serutuf.

The group of four walked along the edge of the ship and looked down. It seemed as deep as a canyon to Sam and Jamie.

"How do we get down there?" asked Jamie.

We jump, said Erar, and she proceeded to demonstrate before Sam could stop her. "Erar! No!" yelled Sam.

But to his surprise, Erar landed softly on the ground and waited for the others to follow.

"How did she...?" Sam started.

"Do you guys have floating abilities?" asked Jamie. "Because we don't have that."

Floating? No. There is nothing supernatural about leaping to the ground. Just science, said Serutuf.

"What science?" Jamie asked.

Our size ratio in relativity to gravity's pull is non-hazardous.

"I think I see what Serutuf is saying. Because we're so small, we won't have much impact from this height," said Sam.

Exactly. Now let's go, said Serutuf, as he threw himself off the ship to land safely near Erar.

"Ok, your turn," Jamie said to Sam.

"I really don't think we have anything to be afraid of.

Let's jump at the same time," said Sam

Jamie was comfortable with this idea and on the count of three they both jumped off the ship. Time stood still; almost as if everything were frozen.

A few seconds later, they were on the ground with the others.

"That was awesome!" said Sam.

"Almost like we're superheroes," added Jamie.

Ok, Sam, you can lead the way, said Serutuf.

Sam looked around. Even though it was his familiar basement, it suddenly appeared foreign territory with this new perspective. Giant paperclips, a giant ball and a huge coin were some of the enormous objects surrounding them. The chairs and tables towered above them like skyscrapers. The stairs leading into the house seemed to go on forever. This was not going to be an easy task – not in the least.

"Uh, Sam, this might be an impossible climb at our size," said Jamie.

Chapter Six

Giants

"We need to get up those stairs somehow," Sam said to Serutuf and Erar. "Can you make us big again? I think we need to be normal size to do this."

We cannot, said Erar. *It takes much less energy to reduce you in size but much more to enlarge you. We do not have sufficient energy available.*

"But it will take forever to climb those stairs," said Jamie.

Then we'll climb the wall, said Serutuf. *Remember, at our size, many things are possible.*

Serutuf demonstrated by grabbing the craggy side of the wall and, remarkably, climbing it. The walls surface had enough bumps and divots to easily grab hold and pull across, much like a bug.

"Wow, incredible!" said Jamie.

And even if you happen to fall, you will not get hurt. You just pick yourself back up, said Erar, as she followed Serutuf.

Sam and Jamie followed. They were very tentative at first, but it was easier than the thought. It was as if they clung to the walls without any effort. It was a fairly quick climb to the top.

The basement door was closed but that didn't matter – the gap at the bottom was large enough to pass through. Now they were in the main house.

"Wow! Everything is so huge! It makes me dizzy seeing everything from this size," said Jamie.

"I know what you mean. I can't even look up," said Sam.

"Thank goodness you don't have carpet," said Jamie, "We'd get lost in it."

We must hurry, said Erar, breaking up Sam and Jamie's conversation.

"Ok. Let's go," said Sam.

They walked along the floor of the long hallway – Even though it was Sam's home, in its gigantic size everything looked foreign.

They finally came to a doorway and Sam stopped.

"This is Gramps' room. The gold coins are in his desk."

They marched across the room to arrive at an old oak roll-top desk. It towered over them, but Sam knew it wouldn't be a problem climbing it. The problem would be getting inside the drawer to get to the coins in question. There didn't appear to be any cracks to crawl through.

"I don't know how we'll get inside," said Sam.

"Which drawer are the coins in?" asked Jamie.

"The top one," said Sam.

"Then there's our solution," she said.

"The top drawer has a keyhole. We can just go through that."

"Yeah. That does look like an option," said Sam.

Off they went – easily climbing the foot and onto the desk itself. The moisture from their hands had almost a sticky effect and it was incredibly fun to pretend they were Spider-man.

Once they reached the keyhole, each one took a turn climbing inside where they found it to be extremely dark.

"We can't see a thing in here. How are we gonna find our way to the coins?" said Sam.

You cannot see? said Erar. We did not realize some of your human limitations.

"So, you can see in the dark?" asked Jamie.

Yes. Our vision adjusts to every light source, or lack thereof. But don't worry, I think we can help you.

To Sam and Jamie's amazement, Erar's body lit up like a blue-green light stick.

"Wow. That is awesome!" said Sam.

The glow of light emanating from Erar filled the drawer space and Sam could now see everything – including the can of coins Gramps had stashed away in the corner.

"There they are!" said Sam.

They walked up to the cache of coins only to wonder how to get them out of there – much less trying to fit them through a small keyhole.

"Hmm. I keep forgetting about our size. Do you have any magic tricks up your sleeve for getting them out of here?" said Sam.

There is a way, said Serutuf.

Serutuf climbed the can and located the gold coins stacked haphazardly inside. He reached inside his body and pulled out a tiny silver device, aimed it at the gold coin and a laser beam cut a huge (to them) chunk out of it. He repeated this procedure two more times and then took the chunks of gold and placed it and the laser device back inside of his body.

Sam and Jamie were still getting used to seeing the aliens do abnormal tricks.

Erar explained, *I know this seems very strange to you humans, but we are transient beings – meaning our bodies are also a vessel to a time-space portal. We can retrieve and send objects within our astral make-up.*

This didn't make any sense to Sam and Jamie of course, but after all, these were aliens – it wasn't supposed to make any sense.

When Serutuf joined them again, Sam asked, "that was all the gold you needed?"

Yes. It is sufficient for now. Later, we can replicate it to make more as needed. It will be enough to fuel our ship and return home.

The group made their way back through the keyhole and down the desk where Sam's dog, Peaches, was waiting for them.

"Oh no – look!" said Jamie.

All four froze as the giant dog walked over to them sniffing away.

"Peaches, it's me! Don't eat us!" Sam pleaded.

Peaches leaned in closer and kept sniffing. She must have recognized Sam's scent because she started wagging her tail. She had no intention of harming them.

Peaches barked happily and then tried to lick Sam.

"Peaches, No!" said Sam, sensing what she was trying to do.

Peaches then crouched into a playful position. Before any of them could react, she flipped on her back and rolled right over them.

When Peaches pulled back upright Sam, Jamie, Serutuf, and Erar found themselves clinging to her back.

"How come we're not dead?" asked Jamie, "I didn't feel a thing!"

Sam and Jamie were becoming more and more accustomed to the incredible abilities they had as a much smaller version of themselves.

They all appeared to be unhurt but now they were sitting on the back of Sam's dog.

"Here, Peaches!" someone called out.

Peaches went flying down the hallway and around the corner, skidding a bit on the hardwood floor. Sam's mom was calling her to go outside.

"Good dog, Peaches. When you're all done you can come back inside."

Sam looked up to see his giant of a mom opening the back door.

"Mom! Help!" yelled Sam.

"Mom!!"

But he knew there was no way his mom could hear his tiny little voice. Besides Peaches was already outside and onto the grass.

She sniffed around a little bit and then relieved herself.

"We need her to go back inside. She could be out here forever," said Jamie.

"Peaches – go get your toy, girl. Let's go!" said Sam hoping to entice his dog back to the house.

Peaches did perk up and started wagging her tail. Her hearing was much better than any human's.

"It's working! Say it again," said Jamie.

But before he could coax her, Peaches turned and shook – violently sending all four passengers scattering in every direction. She took off running and disappeared back inside the house.

Sam landed somewhere among the blades of grass. He knew they were in serious trouble.

"Jamie!" he called out.

Sam righted himself and walked over to where he thought Jamie had landed.

A few more calls.

"Jamie!"

"Jamie!!"

"I'm over here."

Sam climbed over large boulder-sized rocks (which were actually tiny pebbles) and shoved aside large blades of grass and weeds to find Jamie sprawled out on the ground.

"Are you ok?" said Sam.

"I think so. What happened?"

"Peaches shook all of us off her back. We have to find Serutuf and Erar and get back to the house."

"Are you sure you're ok?"

"Yeah. Just getting my bearings. I'll never get used to this size."

"I know what you mean," said Sam, "I keep expecting pain when I fall, and nothing happens."

"I'm not complaining or anything, I just..." Sam trailed off as he spotted something just beyond where Jamie was standing. A monster with giant jaws was barreling straight towards them.

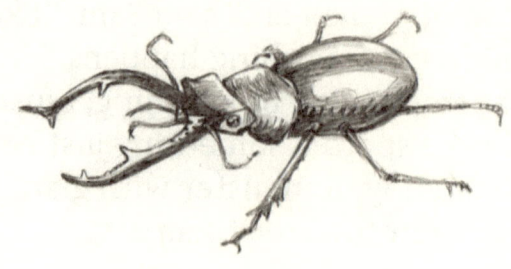

Chapter Seven

Bugged out

Jamie didn't even have time to see the creature, much less react.

Using its gaping jaws, the giant bug scooped her up in a flash.

Jamie screamed.

"Jamie!" Sam ran after the beast which had turned and quickly ran off with its prize.

Sam pushed himself as hard and as fast as he could to catch up to the bug. He barely managed to grab onto one of its many legs and held on for dear life.

The creature crawled for an eternity before finally coming to a stop. Sam could not see Jamie from his position and was horrified to think what it might do to her.

The bug crept up to a huge hole in the ground and released Jamie. She was still screaming as she fell through.

Sam jumped off the bug before it turned and headed off in another direction.

*

Jamie landed on very soft, very squishy ground. When she let her eyes adjust to the darkness, she discovered, to her horror, that she was dropped in a pile of giant bug eggs. Each one was squirming and shifting, generating a disturbing and sickening noise.

Jamie quickly realized that she would be food for these soon-to-be hatching critters. She needed to find a way out before that could happen.

She stumbled across the mound of eggs, looking up to find the entry hole, but it was too far to reach.

It was very claustrophobic and dark. She looked around to find something – anything to use to reach the top but she came up empty.

One of the egg sacs rolled on its side and started to pulse.

"Oh God," said Jamie, as she started to panic. The sac burst open and Jamie couldn't help but scream.

The ugliest-looking bug oozed out and was immediately drawn to the noise. It already had formed pincers which were moving back and forth. No doubt about it, it wanted nourishment.

Its eyes were opaque white indicating that it could not see – that would develop at a later stage. However, its sense of smell was fully functional, and it was zeroing in on tasty human!

Jamie slipped as she tried to run away and that made it much easier for the critter to catch up to her.

Just as it was ready to strike, another baby bug burst through its cocoon and quickly bumped Jamie's attacker off the mound.

Jamie was safe only for a split second.

"Jamie! Here – grab hold of this!" Sam yelled down into the hole. He had gathered enough vine and string to throw down there.

Jamie grabbed the rope and pulled herself up so fast, she surprised herself. She wouldn't know that she barely escaped the baby bug lunging at her heels.

Now she was back on safe ground with Sam.

"Sam, thank God! I owe you one," said Jamie.

"Let's get out of here before they learn how to climb," said Sam.

Quickly, they dashed off and didn't stop until they knew that they were far enough out of danger.

"We have to get back to the house before we run into more bugs," said Jamie.

"I know, but first we have to find Serutuf and Erar," said Sam.

"They could be anywhere," said Jamie.

"We'll find them," Sam said.

They walked on, careful to survey their surroundings and quietly enough so they didn't attract any attention.

"I had no idea your backyard could be so dangerous.

It's like we're in another world," said Jamie.

"Maybe we should grab sharp sticks to use for weapons," said Sam.

There were plenty of sticks to choose from and they both found one suitable for the job. They weren't quite sharp enough, so they filed the ends on a rough rock to make them nice and pointed.

"Do you think they're looking for us too?" asked Jamie. "What if a bug found them first? What if...?" Jamie trailed off, but Sam knew what she meant.

"They'll be fine. They're aliens after all and they probably have built-in weapons," said Sam, thinking of the laser Serutuf used to cut into the gold coin.

"Hey, look!" Jamie pointed.

Sam turned to see a small bellow of smoke just northeast of where they were.

"Come on!" said Sam.

They both ran toward the smoke signal. They figured it was the aliens brilliant way of contacting them. Sam considered the irony of how primitive this idea was in contrast to sophisticated futuristic beings. In any case, it was effective.

Sam and Jamie were getting closer. They sped through the backyard 'forest'...until they came across a lizard standing between them and their destination. The giant lizard looked remarkably like a dinosaur.

"There's no way we can let that thing see us," said Sam.

"It's right in our path," said Jamie.

"Let's wait a bit and see if it leaves," said Sam.

So, they waited...

and waited.

But the lizard wasn't going anywhere.

"Ok, this is not working. We have to scare it away," said Sam.

"Scare it away? Have you seen how small we are?" said Jamie.

"Then we could try to walk clear around it but that will take a while," said Sam.

"No – I think I know what we can try," said Jamie.

"What?" said Sam.

"Camouflage."

"What do you mean?"

"My Dad taught me all about it. When he would go to photograph animals, he wore clothes to blend in with the scenery, so the animals wouldn't even know he was there. Sometimes he would add leaves and stuff to it as well" said Jamie.

"Let's give it a try," said Sam.

They gathered leaves and grass and sticks and covered themselves as best they could from head to toe. After checking to make sure they were fully covered, they were ready to move on.

They slowly crept around the side of the enormous lizard, which noticed movement but didn't respond. Sam and Jamie tried to make as little noise as possible.

So far, the plan was working. They managed to get by the lizard and continue their search for their alien friends.

Closer and closer they progressed to the plume of smoke when they suddenly began to hear Serutuf and Erar. Not audibly, but in their heads.

Very good to see you both in one piece, said Erar, *We were hopeful that our signal would reconnect us.*

"That was a smart idea, Erar. It might never have been possible to find you without it," said Jamie.

Serutuf extinguished the fire and they began to plot their way back to the house.

"We have to avoid being eaten by all the creatures lurking around here," said Sam.

If we stick together and keep our wits, we should be fine, said Serutuf.

They started on their way back and kept on the lookout for predators. It wasn't long before they encountered another giant lizard. It was standing there frozen like a statue. Sam and Jamie wondered if it was the same one or were there many more.

"These are the creatures I was talking about," said Sam, "You guys have to cover yourselves with leaves and grass, so it won't see us."

No, said Serutuf, *There is a better way.*

Serutuf walked right up to the lizard and stood to examined it. Sam was sure he would be eaten alive any second. But something unusual happened.

Ok, Jamie and Sam - climb on its back, said Serutuf.

"What? No way. Do you know what these things do to small critters like us? They *eat* them," said Sam.

Not this one, said Erar. *Serutuf has complete control of its mind.* It will obey his every command.

"Are you positive? That thing is pretty massive," said Jamie.

Yes. Please trust us. It is our fastest way back to your house, said Erar.

Sam and Jamie cautiously approached the beast and began to ascend its tail. Once they were all on top, Serutuf gave the command for it to run to the house.

It was surprisingly fun – almost like an amusement park ride come to life. They were now able to see above the tall grass and the ride itself was fairly smooth.

Every so often the lizard would stop and look around and then start up again. It didn't take very long before they were at the steps of the back porch. They descended the tail and the lizard strode off back in the direction of the grass.

"That was incredible, Serutuf. Can you do that with everyone?" asked Sam, a little concerned that his mind could be broken into.

No. Just beings who do not have rational thought. If we attempted that on a rational being, the connection would kill us both.

In some sense, this gave Sam some comfort.

"Ok, back in the house we go."

Chapter Eight

Home Grown

It was easy for the group to enter the house through the crack at the bottom door. Sam and Jamie were very happy to be back on safe territory.

They walked across the kitchen floor where Sam's mom was preparing some food. Into the hallway and back through the door of the basement. They descended the stairs and headed straight for the ship.

Once they crawled to the top and into the dome, Serutuf and Erar guided them back into the control room.

I will introduce the gold units into the reactor and once we power up, we can transform you both back to your normal size, said Serutuf.

This was music to their ears because while it was a

remarkable experience being the size of a bean, Sam and Jamie thoroughly missed being their human size.

Serutuf walked over to a containment panel and pressed a button. The panel slid open and Serutuf retrieved the three pieces of gold from his celestial body and placed them inside. After closing the panel, he moved over to a control table and pressed several more buttons. The ship started to hum.

Thank you both very much for your much-needed assistance including waking us from hibernation. We owe you a debt of gratitude, said Erar.

"You're welcome. It was a great experience," said Jamie.

Now, let us go back to the dome and restore you to your normal size, said Erar.

Sam, Jamie, and Erar walked back to the dome while Serutuf stayed at the control board to prep.

Are you both ready? asked Erar.

"Yes," they both said.

Goodbye, friends.

Erar gave Serutuf the signal and instructed Sam and Jamie to walk through the glass. As they did, they could feel themselves getting larger. It was the strangest sensation – one that forced them to close their eyes to avoid this disorienting effect.

When they opened their eyes again, they were fully back to normal. it still took them a while to adjust to the pull of gravity.

"Hey, what about the ship? We'll have to bring it back outside," said Jamie.

Jamie spoke prematurely as the ship, without warning, rose up and flung itself at the upper wall of the basement, passing right through it.

"Wow!" said Sam.

Sam and Jamie stood there watching for a few moments, not quite being able to comprehend the events of the last few hours.

"Are we going to tell anybody?" asked Jamie.

"Who's going to believe us?" replied Sam.

"Maybe Gramps," said Jamie.

"What are you going to do with this equipment?" she asked, turning her attention to the receiver that initially brought them in contact with Shrad and the aliens.

"Well, definitely unplugging it, for one. I don't want to have any more conversations with Shrad," said Sam.

Sam pulled the plug out of the wall outlet and they headed upstairs.

When they walked into the living room, Gramps was already sitting in his chair with Penny on his lap. Peaches was laying on the floor beside them and when she saw Sam and Jamie, she raised up and gave a little bark – her tail in motion.

Gramps looked over at them and you could see the relief spread across his face.

"Where have you two been? I was worried sick about you guys getting lost or in trouble."

"We're fine, Gramps. We hiked over to the area where you said you saw something crash," said Sam.

"And guess what? We found a ship!" said Jamie.

"A spaceship," said Sam.

"Hogwash," said Gramps.

'hogwash? What the heck is that supposed to mean?' thought Jamie.

"You didn't find no ship," Gramps clarified.

"Well, we'll tell you all about it later. We have to get cleaned up," said Sam. He continued -

"Is dinner ready? We're starved!"

"Dinner? Dinner won't be ready for another couple of hours," said Gramps.

"Then we'll grab some snacks," said Sam

*

Dinner was possibly the best meal Sam and Jamie had eaten in their life. It was a fairly simple one – roasted potatoes, carrots, chicken and sweet bread. But something about being reduced to half an inch in size and then back again really enhanced their appetite.

"Thanks, Mom. That was awesome," said Sam.

"It was very good, Aunt Sue," added Jamie.

"Thank you. You guys really devoured it. Hiking must have made you both very hungry!" said Mrs Orzabal.

After the meal was finished, Sam and Jamie did their part to help clean the table and wash the dishes.

They went back into the living room where Gramps was sitting in his favorite chair, waiting for them.

"Ok, Gramps, you won't believe what happened to us today..." Sam started.

Sam and Jamie told Gramps everything that

happened after they left to investigate the crash.

"So, you dug up the spaceship and brought it down to the basement?" asked Gramps.

"Yes. And then we were shrunk down to their size to get inside of the ship," said Sam.

"I went down there to look for you guys – I did see a spaceship, but I thought it was one of your model kits. You kids weren't around but you left all that equipment on. I told you about wasting electricity," said Gramps.

"So you *did* cut off Shrad's communication for us. Gramps, you may not know it, but you saved us," said Sam.

"I think you were both out in the sun too long," Gramps said.

"No, Gramps. We can prove it – we made our way to your desk and the aliens cut out a few holes in one of your gold coins," said Jamie.

Gramps arched his brow, "Why were you guys foolin' around in my desk?"

After telling Gramps more details, he seemed to be starting to believe them.

"Well, it's getting late, said Gramps, "I better get to bed."

"Goodnight, Gramps," they said.

"Goodnight. Don't let any more aliens inside," said Gramps, smiling as he headed off to his bedroom.

Sam rolled his eyes.

"I don't think he believes us," said Sam.

"*I* don't even believe us," said Jamie.

Jamie still had three more days to stay at Sam's house. She wasn't sure if she'd be able to sleep well that night, after everything that had happened. She and Sam couldn't stop talking about it. It was just so crazy – like a story they might read in a book.

"Do you think Serutuf and Erar made it back to their galaxy yet?" asked Jamie.

"If they haven't, they're certainly a lot closer by now," said Sam.

"Maybe I'll wake up tomorrow and it will all have been a dream," said Jamie.

"Ha! What fun would that be?" said Sam. "Goodnight – see you in the morning."

"Not if I see you first."

*

The next couple of days were fairly uneventful – just a lot of lounging around, watching television and playing outside. The weather had vastly improved from Jamie's first day. Now, there were hardly any clouds in the sky and the temperature was somewhere in the 70's. Jamie only had one more day to spend with Sam before she had to return home. They had planned to camp out in the backyard and stargaze.

When night approached, Sam and Jamie were all set with their sleeping bags and snacks. It would be the perfect opportunity to look for any flying saucers.

When they finally settled in, they were greeted by

chirping crickets, a slight warm breeze and the most dazzling light show put on by every star in the sky. It was the perfect end to Jamie's visit.

"Man, I have a new appreciation for all the planets and stars out there," said Jamie.

"I can't believe how bright everything is," said Sam, "There's the big dipper!"

"Look – there's the little dipper!"

Sam and Jamie were mesmerized.

There were plenty of shooting stars. Some of which they entertained the possibility of being spaceships. Nothing seemed too far-fetched for them now.

Eventually, like reading a good book at night, the light show started to put them to sleep.

"'Night, Jamie. See you in the morning."

"Not if I see you first."

Sam smiled and fell into a restful slumber.

PART II

Chapter Nine

Revisiting

Sam...we have unfinished business...

Sam grimaced and tried to get comfortable, but something was preventing that from happening.

Sam...wake up...

Sam opened his eyes and tried to transition from dream to reality. When he finally pulled himself out of sleep, he noticed that he was surrounded by large floating material – large leaves, bits of paper – as far as the eyes could see. He stumbled through the billowing material and couldn't get his balance.

Then he saw it – right above him was a shiny, suspended metal craft with flickering lights. Sam quickly realized that this giant pillar of cloth was his sleeping bag. He had been reduced, once again, to the size of a peanut.

'Oh no,' he thought. His first reaction was to locate Jamie. But before that could happen, an amber-colored beam of light came from above and started to pull Sam upward.

"Sam!"

Sam looked over his shoulder and could see Jamie being lifted into the air as well. They were both being abducted by this familiar alien spaceship.

"Jamie, are you ok?" asked Sam.

"Yes, but what the hell is happening?" she said.

By this time, the beam had already pulled them into the hull of the ship.

"I thought I was dreaming at first," said Jamie.

"For some reason, Serutuf and Erar came back for us," said Sam.

"What? Why?"

"I guess we'll find out soon enough," said Sam as a door panel opened to reveal...

"Erar! Serutuf!" They both exclaimed.

Please accept our apologies for your capture, said Erar.

"Capture? What do you mean?" asked Sam.

We had no choice, said Erar.

"That is correct, they are only obeying my orders," said a voice from nowhere but everywhere at once.

It was an all-too familiar voice. One that evoked a sense of dread among the cousins.

"Shrad!" said Sam.

"What do you want with us?" asked Jamie.

"I am not one to leave a project behind. You two were intended to be my captors. I have great plans for you humans."

Jamie shivered at the thought of being some kind of pet for a disturbed alien.

"I can't believe this," said Sam, "Serutuf, is there anything you can do?"

I am sorry, Sam. We are at Shrad's mercy. As long as he can monitor our ship, he has the ability to disintegrate it. We have no choice but to follow his commands.

"That's correct, and obey you will," said Shrad from somewhere overhead.

"I need that gold to be replicated for our own use. In addition to that, I also need human specimens."

"Is that what we are? Nothing but trophies?" Jamie questioned, now with fire in her voice. "I thought advanced species would be more logical and compassionate," she continued.

Sam was a little surprised by Jamie's outburst.

"You would do well to watch yourself, human. If you need to blame someone for your predicament, look no further than yourself. You are the ones who freed the aliens and enabled your capture," said Shrad.

"But be assured – you will do a great service to my people. We have lots of experiments in mind for you in the name of science."

"But enough of this conversation – please prepare yourselves to be transferred to my ship."

With that, Shrad cut his communication.

Sam, Jamie. We can fully communicate through thought. Don't try to speak verbally, said Erar.

Sam and Jamie did as she instructed and proceeded to 'talk' to the aliens without speaking.

We can't let Shrad do this, said Sam.

For now, we must do as he says, said Serutuf. *But we do have a plan and need your help to carry it out.*

Sam and Jamie were relieved to know that Erar and Serutuf were not just going to hand them over to a sinister alien race.

We will carry it out once we dock inside of their spaceship, continued Serutuf.

Once they were finished discussing the plans to overtake Shrad, Serutuf and Erar concentrated on managing the controls of the ship. Sam and Jamie continued the conversation.

"Sam, I really hope this works. What if we never make it back?" said Jamie.

"Don't even put that thought in your mind," said Sam. "It's gonna work – we have Serutuf and Erar on our side."

The ship continued speeding toward their destination. Serutuf and Erar informed them that they would arrive within the hour. For the rest of the trip, no one said much. The only thought was to get back to Earth.

Forty-five minutes later, Erar broke the silence.

There is his ship.

Sam and Jamie could see the vessel on one of the monitor screens and it was impressive. It was not the simple, small metal ship they were riding in, but a large, gray model with multiple layers and plenty of flashing, multi-colored lights.

As they moved closer, the image grew bigger – until

they were close enough to be underneath the craft. It was behemoth.

The bottom section opened to reveal a huge, gaping hole which swallowed up their ship. It was an ominous feeling to board the unknown, and Sam and Jamie were understandably nervous.

Ok, do not forget what we discussed; but we must wait for the right time, said Serutuf.

We'll be ready, Jamie said in thought.

When the ship was stationary, the crew was instructed to exit and wait further instructions.

All four walked off their ship and into their captor's vessel. It was wide open and barren. The lights were bright and accusing. All they could do now was wait.

It did not take long for a figure to emerge from one of the wall panels. This figure was large and imposing. He was wearing green flowing material which seemed to move of its own accord. His expression was vacant, with his large black eyes, a snout, and what looked like a proboscis for a mouth.

"Greetings, guests. I am Shrad," it said.

Shrad was five times as tall as his captives, which still meant he was tiny compared to normal human size.

"What do you plan to do with us?" asked Jamie, who was keen to find out her fate.

"For now, you and Sam are my special guests who will enjoy the amenities of my ship. Please, all of you, follow me."

Shrad turned and led them back through the open door panel. Sam and Jamie wondered when they were going to initiate 'the plan' to overtake Shrad. It would have to be later.

Shrad took them down a very plain corridor and into a maze of tunnels. If you weren't familiar with the layout, you would get lost in an instant.

No one spoke even though there were plenty of questions to be asked.

They finally made their way into an opening and Sam and Jamie were very surprised by what they saw.

It was beautiful – the exact replica of Earth's landscape. There were trees, lakes, waterfalls, birds were chirping. The sky was the perfect shade of blue. Scattered throughout the landscape were beautiful cottage-style houses with inviting, manicured lawns.

"Are we back on Earth?" Jamie asked, hopefully.

"You are not," said Shrad. "This is part hologram, part replicated materials to make you both feel at home. You have your choice of any of the houses where you should be able to sleep comfortably. Also, you will find inside each house a sustenance machine for whichever food items you wish. You will be grateful to me for providing you with this utopian life."

"I don't think so," said Jamie, "It's not Earth. It's not real."

Shrad gazed at her and said nothing. Instead, he turned to Serutuf and Erar, "Come. We have business to discuss. The humans can take some time to explore their new surroundings."

With that, Shrad, Serutuf and Erar walked away leaving Sam and Jamie alone in this horribly fake Earth.

Chapter Ten

Fellow Prisoners

"I would like for you to transfer the formula for the Earth's gold."

Shrad was now addressing Serutuf and Erar in one of the many rooms on this ship.

We are prepared to give you the formula, said Erar, *but we would like to negotiate the return of the humans to earth.*

"Sadly, you are in no position for negotiations. If you do not comply with my demands, you will find yourselves prisoners until my request is satisfied," said Shrad.

What are your plans for the humans? asked Serutuf.

"I'm sure you already know – they will be studied for science and then after, dissected for further research."

These words immediately brought a sense of despair to Erar and Serutuf. They were resolute in putting their plan in motion to avoid that scenario.

*

"I wonder what they're doing right now?" said Sam.

The cousins were wandering in their new environment, secretly amazed at how realistic it felt. The grass rustled in the wind, the water in the lakes gently rippled, the birds darted from tree to tree. If they didn't think about it, they would feel as if they were back on Earth. However, this place was as foreign as the moon.

"Serutuf and Erar wouldn't abandon us, would they?" asked Jamie.

"I don't think so," was all Sam could say. He didn't have the heart to say that it was a possibility.

As they continued wandering the field, Jamie saw movement in the distance.

"Sam, look!"

Jamie was pointing at something just beyond the shrouded horizon. Sam observed two kids walking toward them.

"Hey, look! Two other humans!" said Sam.

They all ran to meet each other with exuberant

greetings.

"Wow! How did you guys get here? Were you captured by Shrad too? Where on earth are you from? (no pun intended)."

It took them a little while to calm down from the excitement of seeing one of their own so far from home.

"I'm Steven and this is my sister, Janice," said the boy.

Steven looked to be a little younger than Sam – maybe around twelve. He had long hair, blue eyes and was wearing jeans and a t-shirt. His sister, Janice, looked a couple of years younger than her brother. She had the same blue eyes and her sandy blonde hair was pulled back into a ponytail. She was wearing a white dress with floral patterns.

"We were both asleep in our beds and when we awoke, we were aboard this ship. The alien told us that we were brought here as a service to his alien race," said Steven, "We've been here for almost a week. You're the first humans we've seen since then."

"We were captured too," said Jamie, "We're trying to figure out a way to get back."

"It doesn't seem possible. We've pleaded with that alien to bring us back to Earth, but he just tells us this is our new home," said Steven.

"Not if we can help it," said Sam, "We're working on a plan that just might get us out of here. We have two friendly aliens working to free us," said Jamie.

Steven and Janice looked hopeful.

During the next hour Steven and his sister gave Sam and Jamie a tour of the land. Even though they were on an otherworldly ship, the atmosphere of 'Earth' did comfort them. It was meticulously created, even down to the flying birds and butterflies.

Some of the houses embellishing the landscape had swing sets, some had pools, some were two-story, and some were single-story homes. Each one was perfectly landscaped.

"Where do you sleep? In one of those houses?" asked Sam.

"Yeah. You can choose any house you like. They're all open and they have beds and bathrooms and things," said Steven.

"They also have a kitchen that can create any food you like."

"Let's check one out," said Jamie, "I'm super thirsty. Do they have water?"

"Water, juice, coke. Whatever you ask for, it will give it to you," replied Steven.

All four approached the nearest house and went inside. It was beautifully furnished and looked just like an ordinary home on Earth.

They walked through the living room and into the kitchen. Steven walked over to a device on the wall that had a few buttons and a grid.

"What would you like to drink?" asked Steven.

"Can I get a lemonade?" said Jamie.

Steven pushed one of the button and it lit up. He spoke 'lemonade' into the grid and there was a small hum of noise behind the wall indicating it had received the order. Fifteen seconds later a sliding panel opened to reveal a frosty cold glass of lemonade.

Jamie reached out and took it and slowly brought it to her mouth.

"Is it safe to drink?" she said.

"Yes. I've never had any problem with their food or drinks," reassured Steven.

Jamie took a small sip. It was perfect. She allowed herself to gulp it down and said, "That has got to be the best glass of lemonade I've ever tasted."

Sam couldn't wait to get his. He punched the button and spoke, 'lemonade'. In a few seconds, out came a second glass of the most amazing tasting lemonade.

"This really is incredible," said Sam.

"Yeah, you get used to it after a few days, then it becomes the norm," said Steven.

After a few glasses, they wanted to look through the rest of the house.

They walked into the living room and down the hallway. There was a bathroom and four bedrooms. The bedroom had inviting beds, a desk a lamp and nothing at all to make it seem like they were thousands of miles away from their home planet.

When they finished the tour of the house, it didn't take long for the conversation to return to their alien abductor.

"Has Shrad done anything to hurt you?" asked Jamie, concerned about them both but mostly for Steven's sister, Janice who hadn't said much since they met.

"No. He has left us alone for the most part," said Steven, "Occasionally he summons us to ask questions and take computer readings from a weird machine. Then he'll ask us if we have any questions or concerns and then he lets us come back here."

"Hopefully, you won't have to deal with that ever again. We'll stick together from here on out and keep working to get back to our real home," said Sam.

"Let's go back outside and look around some more. I'm hoping we'll hear from Serutuf and Erar soon."

*

Shrad led Serutuf and Erar back to their ship to retrieve what he brought them here for – gold.

"Just send the chemical compound code of the gold to the ship's computer, as well as a piece of the gold itself, and then you are free to leave," said Shrad.

When Serutuf and Erar entered their own ship, they immediately began plotting.

We need to get Sam and Jamie back to our ship to put the plan in motion, said Erar.

Yes, but we also need to have Shrad here as well. This will take some planning. We will delay departure until then, said Serutuf.

Serutuf walked over to the control panel to pull up the gold formula. When that was done, he retrieved the piece of gold and exited the ship.

Shrad was waiting outside as he was much too large to fit inside of their ship. He would never allow being reduced to their size.

"Ah, thank you for your service," said Shrad as he accepted the tiny bit of gold.

We have transferred the chemical code of the gold's make-up to your ship's computer, said Serutuf.

"Very good," said Shrad, "You are free to go."

We can't leave just yet, said Erar.

"Oh?"

We would like to give our farewells to the humans, said Erar.

"Really? You have grown fond of them in your short time together?" Shrad laughed. It was an, insulting laugh, mocking the aliens who would show signs of compassion for lowly humans.

"Fine – they are out exploring their 'Earth' environment. You may seek them out. I have more important matters to tend to." Shrad slithered away, not bothering to lead them to Sam and Jamie. Serutuf and Erar had been hoping he would summon them. It would have fit their plans perfectly. But they were not deterred and started on their way to find them.

*

Sam, Jamie, Steve, and Janice walked across a small bridge above a running stream. It was a beautiful scene but at the same time a cruel reminder of their real homeworld.

"There are lots of streams and lakes. Some of them even have fish," said Steven.

"There are also apple trees and peach trees scattered around. The fruit tastes just like the ones back home," he continued.

"I've got to hand it to Shrad – he went all out trying to get us used to this place. I hate to tell him that it ain't gonna work," said Sam.

They walked for a while until they came across one of the apple trees. They stopped to sample the fruit. It was delicious, of course.

"What's this plan you've been talking about? How are you going to stop Shrad from keeping us here?" asked Steven.

"Well, it involves our alien friends increasing our size so we can contain Shrad and ultimately sabotage his ship's computer. I imagine we'll have to be near their ship and ready when they give us the signal," said Jamie.

"Yes, Serutuf told us that Shrad cannot be reduced or enlarged, only humans. He'll be no match for us at that size," added Sam.

"I like that plan," said Steven, but what about me and Janice? What are we supposed to do?"

"Nothing. Just keep back and let us carry it out," said Jamie.

They continued to walk, with Steven showing them some of the areas he was familiar with. Jamie stayed close to Janice, noticing she had been very quiet the whole time.

"How are you holding up so far?" Jamie asked Janice.

"I'm ok. I just miss my family so much," she replied sadly.

"I know. But we'll be back home soon, I promise,"

Jamie reassured her. "You have your brother, and now you have us," Jamie smiled.

"Aren't you afraid?" said Janice

"Yes. I'm very afraid. But you can't let fear stop you from doing the things you need to do. I use fear as motivation," said Jamie.

"I'm glad you're here with us. I feel so much better," said Janice.

They continued exploring the gardens, the wildlife and other surroundings, but now the group was getting tired.

"I say we head back to the houses and get something to eat and then try to get some sleep," said Sam, "It doesn't look as if our friends are going to meet up with us today – but if they do, I want to be ready."

They all agreed and started on their way back to one of the houses.

"I wonder what Mom and Gramps are doing right now?" said Sam.

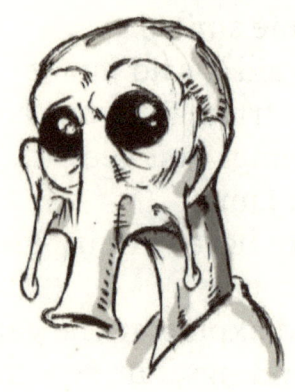

Chapter Eleven

The Incident

"Where can they be?" Mrs. Orzabal was beyond a little concerned. It was 8am, and Sam and Jamie's sleeping bags were vacant.

"They don't normally just up and leave without telling me - and definitely not without eating breakfast. "Dad, I'm worried."

Gramps was enjoying his oatmeal and raisins, with Penny sitting close by his side.

"Don't worry about them, Sue. They're old enough to take care of themselves. They probably just went exploring again."

"I know – and I'm sure they went against my rules not to go looking for that meteor. When they get back, they're gonna get it."

Secretly Gramps was worried too. It wasn't like them to disappear like that. Also, he kept thinking about the story Sam and Jamie told him about the aliens and the spaceship. But that was so far-fetched. Wasn't it?

*

Once the group of four were back in the house, they quickly discovered that they were famished. They headed to the kitchen to order some food. Sam ordered pizza and once Jamie saw how good it looked and smelled, she ordered the same (except with a pineapple topping). Soon they were all eating pizza and discussing the day's events. They even allowed themselves to laugh a bit.

It was starting to get late and everyone was now very tired, so it was suggested they head to bed for the night.

That's when the doorbell rang.

"Who is that? Do you get anyone ringing the doorbell around here?" Sam asked Steven.

"No, this is the first time," Steven replied.

Sam got up and walked over to the door.

"Who is it?"

It is Serutuf and Erar, came the reply – but only in Sam's head.

Sam flung the door open and was happy to see his

alien friends again.

"Serutuf! Erar! Jamie – look they came back for us!"

Jamie was already at the door and hugging them. It was a custom Erar and Serutuf were not privy to, but they understood. They were also happy to see their human friends.

Sam and Jamie invited Serutuf and Erar inside to meet their human friends and to discuss when to carry out the plan.

"This is Steven and Janice," said Sam, "Shrad brought them here as well, but they'll be coming back with us."

Steven and Janice were not too thrilled to meet more aliens, but they knew to keep their composure. Janice kept her distance – standing further back trying not to draw attention to herself.

"Hello," Steven said.

Hello, fellow humans. If everything goes well, you will soon be on your way back to your home planet, said Erar.

"We're all looking forward to that," said Jamie, "The question is – when will that be?"

I would recommend you rest for tonight. We can meet early tomorrow morning and put the plan in motion. We need Shrad to be there as well, said Serutuf.

"How are we going to know when to show up?" asked Sam.

"Also, how are we going to get back to your ship? We could easily get lost," added Jamie.

Take this device, said Serutuf as he pulled out a small silver orb from his body.

This is a tracking device and will point the way to our ship. It will also signal you when we are ready.

Jamie reached out to accept the orb. She was

surprised that it pulsed in her hand, which almost made her drop it. She tucked it away safely in her pocket.

Now we must go back. Get a good night's sleep so you will be ready in the morning, said Erar.

"Ok," said Sam.

Serutuf and Erar walked back outside and headed back to their ship. Sam and Jamie were nervous for the next day but couldn't wait for it to happen.

"Ok, guys, everything is set," Jamie said to Steven and Janice, "I'm hoping tonight's the last night you sleep in this horrible place."

"What was that silver thing the aliens gave you?" asked Janice.

Jamie was surprised that had Janice spoken up.

She reached back into her pocket and pulled out the metal orb. It was silent.

"Serutuf said it is our tracking device. It will lead us to them in the morning."

They all gathered to look at it and feel its smooth, shiny surface. It was definitely not something they were familiar with.

"Well, I'm really tired. I'm going to bed, so I can wake up early. I suggest you guys do the same," said Jamie.

"Agreed. Goodnight, all," said Sam.

The bed was so comfortable that Jamie felt a little guilty for enjoying it. Within mere moments, she was fast asleep. Silence took hold of the house and eventually, they were all asleep.

Jamie's dreams were not very peaceful. She dreamed of being lost in the forest, trying to make her way back home – running feverishly through trees. There was no sign of civilization. She ran for miles before spotting something in the distance. When she made her way closer, she could make out a rudimentary shape. Closer, still, until she was able to discover it was Shrad!

She turned to run but like most dreams, she was only running in place.

Shrad walked closer, reached out his tentacle and said, "you're not going anywhere."

Jamie jolted out of her sleep. She quickly gathered her thoughts and calmed herself down. She needed a drink of water, so she pulled herself out of bed and made her way into the hallway. She peeked in on Sam who was fast asleep. She did the same for Steven and he, too, was soundly sleeping. However, when she checked in on Janice, her bed was empty.

"Janice," she whispered.

No response.

Perhaps she was in the bathroom – but no lights were on in there.

Maybe she went to get a drink of water as well.

Jamie made her way to the kitchen, but Janice was nowhere to be found. She ran back to Sam's room.

"Sam!"

"Sam, wake up!"

Sam scrunched his face and looked at Jamie in a sleep-daze.

"What's up? Did you get a signal from Serutuf?" he asked.

"No. Janice is missing."

"What? She's probably in the bathroom."

"No, I checked everywhere. We have to wake Steven."

Sam and Jamie knocked on Steven's door even

though it was open.

"Steven, wake up," said Sam.

"What's going on?" said Steven.

"Janice is missing – she's not in her bed," said Jamie.

"Oh, she's always doing that. She's probably outside – the stars seem to calm her down."

Steven did not appear too concerned.

"We have to go look for her," said Jamie, "I don't think it's safe for her to be out there by herself."

"Ok, ok. Give me a minute," said Steven.

All three suddenly heard a noise in the front room and Sam and Jamie quickly went to investigate. The front door slowly opened and in walked Janice.

"Janice! You had me worried! Why were you outside in the middle of the night?" asked Jamie.

"I couldn't sleep. Whenever I can't sleep, I go out and look at the stars," said Janice.

"Ok. Well, I hope this will be the last night we spend at this place. Do you want me to sleep in your room tonight?"

"Yes, if you don't mind," said Janice.

"Let's try and get a few more hours of sleep before we have to leave," said Sam.

They all retreated to their rooms except for Jamie who kept Janice company. It wasn't long before they were back to sleep again.

Early the next morning the outside light served as their alarm and slowly broke the group from their slumber. Sam met up with Jamie first to ask about the signal device.

"Anything from our friends?" said Sam.

"Not a word. I thought they wanted to get started

early," said Jamie.

"Maybe early for them is noon," said Sam.

Soon they were all gathered in the living room and discussing how they were going to pull off the escape.

"You guys just stay close," Sam said to Steven and Janice, "and try to stay out of sight. This is a dangerous plan. We don't know what kind of weapons Shrad might have. I'm hoping Erar and Serutuf have already taken that into account."

Jamie had taken the orb out of her pocket and was constantly monitoring it. An hour went by. They were getting antsy.

"Ahh – this waiting is driving me nuts. I'm going to get something to drink," said Sam.

Jamie followed him into the kitchen, leaving Steven and Janice in the living room.

"Orange juice," said Sam.

Within seconds, a tall glass of pristine-looking orange liquid revealed itself from the wall panel.

"I'm a little worried about Janice," said Jamie.

"How come?" Sam asked as he sipped the glass of orange juice.

"Last night she almost looked like she was in a trance and she hasn't said very much since."

"She doesn't say much to begin with," said Sam.

"Yeah but this is different. And Steven doesn't appear to be too worried about her."

"Well, he said she does this all the time. He's probably used to it," said Sam.

"Maybe."

Sam placed his glass down after only drinking half.

"Come on, let's get out of the house. We can think

better outside."

Sam, Jamie, Steven and Janice headed 'outdoors' and watched the sunrise cast ambient shadows across the trees. The temperature was a bit cooler –just like real mornings on Earth. Despite the immaculate appearance of Earth's outdoors, there were in fact a few signs of imperfection – things that were just slightly off, like the fact the butterflies flew in a straight line and that everything was a little too clean, almost sterile.

"Where do these trails lead, Steven?" asked Sam, "have you seen the other side of the hills?"

"No – we don't stray too far from the homes. We didn't want to get lost out there."

"While we're waiting, we can hike up one of the trails and get a bird's-eye view of this place," said Sam.

They hiked a trail leading up a nearby hill and immediately saw that the area they resided in was an enclosure. Just beyond the trees and fields you could see the walls of the enormous ship.

"See! Look over there – you can see where this Earth place ends. It looks like it's miles away but if we were our normal size it would just be a few yards," said Sam.

"Maybe we should start walking until they signal us," said Jamie.

"Good idea. Let's go," said Sam.

The trail was a bit sandy, which was another thing off about this place. They were careful to keep their footing, but Sam stumbled and instinctively reached out to prevent his fall. Unfortunately, Steven was standing right next to him and took an inadvertent shove.

"Oh my God!" yelled Jamie, as Steven lost his footing

and tumbled over the side of the cliff.

"Steven!!" yelled Sam, as he tried to catch him.

It was too late. Steven careened off the cliff and onto several jagged rocks before landing with a solid 'thump' on the ground. Janice must have been in shock because she just stood there silent and motionless.

Sam and Jamie rushed down the hill, afraid of what they knew they would find. What they found was Steven sprawled on the ground – but what they didn't expect to see is what shocked them even more.

Chapter Twelve

I, Spy

Sam and Jamie stood over Steven, unable to make any sense of what they were witnessing.

Metallic parts jutted from Steven's body – gears, springs. No blood – but a green pool of liquid.

"What the hell..?" Sam finally said.

"I don't believe it," said Jamie. "We were played. I just can't believe it!"

"He seemed so real. There was no way we could have known," said Sam.

"Sam, wait a minute – then that must mean..." Jamie didn't have a chance to finish. She was interrupted by Janice.

"That is correct humans. I, too, am an android."

Sam and Jamie turned to see Janice standing behind them, staring her intrusive stare. Except it wasn't Janice's voice anymore. It was Shrad's.

"I needed to check on you without being obvious. It was the only way to receive pertinent information."

Sam immediately thought about what he had told them – everything about their intended plan. Everything about Serutuf and Erar. He felt sick to his stomach.

"I must confine you both to one of the houses until further notice. I am also dealing with your 'friends' appropriately."

Now they felt as helpless as ever. Not only had they revealed their plan of escape, but they had also put Serutuf and Erar in serious danger.

"Now, for you two – please proceed back to the house. Janice will escort you and keep guard until I request your presence."

Janice gestured in the direction of the house and waited for Sam and Jamie to lead the way back. They were in no position to resist, so they did as they were told.

When they reached the front door, Shrad spoke through Janice once again.

"Now relax and get used to the idea that this is now your home. Any attempt to leave will result in your termination. Janice's eyes have the ability to produce a deadly laser which she can fire at will – my will, of course. If I am alerted that you have attempted to escape, I will give the order for her to do so. Have a pleasant rest of the day."

Sam and Jamie entered the house and walked into the living room. Janice remained stationary outside the front door.

"Now what are we going to do? It doesn't look good for us," said Jamie.

"We scout around for another exit," said Sam.

"You know there's only one way out and that's through the front door – it's the only door in this stupid house," said Jamie.

"Maybe we can knock Janice over and run before she has a chance to shoot us," she continued.

"No. That's too risky. Besides, we don't want to alert Shrad that we escaped," said Sam.

"I just can't believe they were robots. They didn't act mechanical at all; and now that I think about it, that explains why Janice disappeared at night – she was probably contacting or reporting to Shrad," said Jamie.

"Poor Serutuf and Erar. I know they'll be punished for this."

A loud *ping* came out of Jamie's pocket.

"Hey, the signal device!" she said.

Jamie pulled it out and it was pulsing and showed a green-pointed indicator.

"Serutuf and Erar must have sent the signal before Shrad got to them," said Sam.

"We have to get out of here and find them," said Jamie.

Sam and Jamie spent the next hour searching the house for an escape and occasionally peeking out the front window, only to see Janice steadfastly standing guard.

"Let's try to break a bedroom window and get out

that way," said Jamie.

"We could try, but it will make noise and probably alert Janice," said Sam.

"If we can muffle the sound somehow, she wouldn't know we broke through," said Jamie.

"Ok. We can try the upstairs back bedroom. She can't see us from there," said Sam.

Sam and Jamie entered the back bedroom and pulled the curtains away from the window. Sam picked up a lamp that was sitting on a desk and rapped it on the window, which proved unshakable. Sam tried to forcefully kick at it a few times to no avail.

"This window is solid. It doesn't look like we can break it. We would need a crowbar or something and even then, it would call too much attention to us," said Sam.

Sam and Jamie had no choice but to go back downstairs and keep searching. Jamie peeked out at Janice once again. Just as before, she was unflinching at guard. Her eyes were trained on the front door – the only exit.

"Jamie, look!" Sam said. He was pointing at the fireplace.

"That's our exit."

They walked over to the fireplace and pulled open the glass door and screen. Sam poked his head inside and looked up to see blue skylight.

"I think we can just fit," he said. "Once we're on top, we can jump down from the back of the house."

"Ok, we've got nothing to lose at this point. You go first," said Jamie as she eyed the small opening to the shaft.

Sam shimmied his way up the opening and was making progress – until he got halfway, then he couldn't move.

"Hey, why'd you stop?" asked Jamie.

"I think I'm stuck!"

"That's what I was afraid of," replied Jamie. "Maybe I can come up and push you through."

"No. Then we'd both be stuck," said Sam.

"Wait – I have an idea," said Jamie as she ran off.

"She'd better not be thinking about starting a fire," Sam mumbled to himself.

In a few minutes, Jamie was back in the living room holding a cup.

"I'm going to fling this at you," she said.

"Fling what?" said Sam.

"Melted butter."

Jamie took the cup of melted butter and tossed it up at Sam as hard as she could.

"Ow!" said Sam.

"Sorry, I just had to make sure it got on you," said Jamie.

After a little bit of squirming, Sam managed to get enough butter on him to start moving again.

"That was good thinking. I think it's going to work," said Sam.

Sam worked his way up the chimney and finally out onto the roof of the house.

"Made it!" he called down, "Now it's your turn."

Jamie started up the shaft but was worried if now the butter made it too slippery for her to climb. She needn't have worried – because the shaft was constructed of large rocks, she had lots of places to grip. Soon she was out on the roof with Sam.

They carefully walked to the back of the house hoping Janice was still keeping watch at the front door. When they arrived at the back of the house they dangled from the edge of the roof and let go to fall safely on the grass.

"We did it!" said Sam in hushed excitement.

"You have the orb signal?"

Jamie pulled the pulsing round object from her pocket to let it lead them to Serutuf and Erar.

"Let's go," said Sam.

They quietly made their way through the yard, around trees and over hills until they arrived at a clearing. They both took a moment to catch their breath.

"I hope they're ok. If Shrad killed them for rebelling, we're lost," said Jamie.

"They *have* to be ok. Once we find them, we'll deal with Shrad," said Sam.

"Come on – it looks like we're back near the entrance to the regular ship rooms."

They entered through the door panel and instantly the illusion of Earth disappeared. Instead, there were the cold, sleek, metallic walls and blinking lights of a vast alien space vessel. They were now that much closer to finding Serutuf and Erar.

The orb which Jamie was holding pulsed faster, and the green arrow pointed the way. They walked down a long, winding corridor with many different paths. Some of the darker halls were nerve-wracking because they couldn't see what was waiting for them. They had put all of their faith and trust in this tiny little gizmo.

The search was taking forever, increasing their already high anxiety levels. They walked until the green arrow pointed to a large door, indicating that they had reached their destination.

"This is it," said Sam. "Serutuf and Erar are behind this door."

"Ok, but how do we get inside?" said Jamie, "There are no handles or buttons."

Sam futilely pushed on the door with no result.

"Now what? Maybe Shrad is the only one who can open it," said Jamie.

"We have to find a way somehow. Maybe we can look around for a button or a hidden panel," said Sam.

The cousins frantically searched for some kind of wall mechanism to open the large door but came up empty. They were at the point of giving up when Jamie had an idea.

"Wait – if Serutuf and Erar *are* behind this door then that means we're close enough to communicate with them."

"Let's try it," said Sam.

"Concentrate. Let's let them know we're here," said Jamie.

Both Sam and Jamie called out to their alien friends through telepathy.

Serutuf!

Erar!

It's Sam and Jamie. Are you in there?

At first, nothing. And then...

Friends...

Sam and Jamie were relieved to get a call back.

Shrad has us as prisoners. We don't have much time, said

Serutuf.

We're right outside the door but we can't find a way to get in, said Sam.

Take the orb and place it up against the door – it will deactivate and open, said Serutuf.

Jamie did as she was instructed, and soon they could hear whirring and clicking sounds within the walls. In moments, the door slid open and Jamie and Sam were horrified by what they saw.

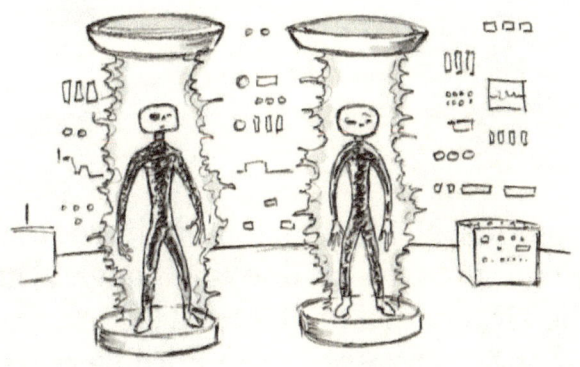

Chapter Thirteen

Energy Crisis

Gramps and Sue Orzabal were now seriously considering calling the authorities. Mrs. Orzabal was a wreck.

"I should call Jamie's father and tell him we're concerned," she said.

"Wait," said Gramps, "I gotta tell you what they told me."

Gramps began to tell his daughter what Sam and Jamie had told him – finding a real spaceship, meeting aliens, shrinking down to half an inch.

Sue Orzabal sat and listened. Then she became concerned about Gramps, too.

*

Sam and Jamie walked into a dimly lit room filled with weird instruments, funny-looking gadgets, and flashing lights. The air smelled of electricity.

Serutuf and Erar were here – both were in frozen suspension inside clear tube cylinders. Both looked near death.

"Oh no! What did Shrad do to you?!" exclaimed Jamie.

We don't have much time, said Serutuf, *he is draining us of all our energy. I hope it is not too late for Erar. Do you see the machine there?*

Serutuf was obviously referring to a massive square console nearby, buzzing with activity.

Place the orb onto the machine and step back.

Jamie did as he asked and suddenly the machine started to smoke. There was a flash of light and Serutuf and Erar tumbled to the ground. Sam and Jamie ran to help them.

"Are you both ok?" Sam asked.

Give me a moment. We need to check on Erar.

Erar was not showing any movement. It did not appear she had any life left.

"Erar! Wake up!" Jamie started shaking her.

She needs energy – help me to her. We have to make contact, said Serutuf.

Sam and Jamie carefully guided Serutuf over to Erar

to join hands. After a while, Serutuf gave them the bad news.

It's no use. I haven't the energy and strength to revive her.

"No! We *have* to keep trying. What if we join hands with you? Would that help?"

I do not know. We have never connected with humans before, said Serutuf.

"Well, we're going to do it now," said Jamie. "Sam, grab Serutuf's hand."

Sam did as she asked while Serutuf held Erar's hand. Jamie grabbed Erar's other hand and then she took hold of Sam's, forming a circle.

Sam and Jamie slowly started to weaken. They felt energy draining from their bodies.

I think it may be working, said Serutuf.

Sam was hoping he didn't pass out. He and Jamie held on as long as they could until...

Thank you, friends.

Erar was conscious. They all released hands and took a moment to recuperate.

Welcome back, Erar, said Serutuf, obviously relieved.

"Yeah, we thought you were a goner," said Jamie.

If it weren't for our human friends offering their energy, you would be, said Serutuf.

I owe you both a debt of gratitude that I will never forget, said Erar.

"We're glad you're ok," said Jamie.

Come, we still have much work to do to defeat Shrad, said Serutuf as he grabbed the signal orb still sitting on the broken console.

They marched off into the corridors and on their way

to find their ship.

*

Serutuf and Erar led the way. They didn't need the orb
to guide them – they were familiar with the way back to
their ship. They knew that Shrad would soon be aware
of their escape and come after them.

It wasn't long before they arrived at the hanger
where the ship was docked. They quickly went over the
plan once again and were now ready to face Shrad.

Serutuf and Erar boarded the ship while Sam and
Jamie stayed behind, all the while remaining in
telepathic contact with them. It was now time to draw
Shrad into the fray.

Serutuf put out the call to summon Shrad and let him
know they were currently in their ship with the
humans.

"Fools!" Shrad was irate. "Do they think I would
allow that?"

Shrad put out a call for Janice and headed for the
hanger. He knew they could not leave without him
opening the hatch.

Shrad swiftly made his way through the corridors. He
did not fear any retaliation because Serutuf and Erar's
ship's weapons were deactivated, and he was much
larger than any of them. He turned down the last
corridor and into the hanger. He was now face to face

with Sam and Jamie.

"You have evaded capture for the last time. I have given you both the best possible living conditions but now that is over."

"We're not intimidated by you, Shrad. In fact, it's you who'll be captured," said Jamie angrily.

"How do you plan to do that, may I ask?" said Shrad, slightly bemused.

"Like this."

Jamie gave a signal and there was a snap of electricity in the air. Both Jamie and Sam were now transforming into larger figures.

"No!" Shrad called out as he turned to run but Sam quickly snapped him up in his now-giant hands.

Serutuf and Erar successfully performed the enlargement procedure – but not to the cousins' full size, or they would outgrow the ship itself. They had enlarged them to one quarter of their normal size – enough to easily overpower Shrad.

"Release me! Release me now!" Shrad screamed.

"Calm down, little alien thing. You're in no position to threaten anyone," said Jamie.

Now, Sam, hold him tight while I go and destroy his ship's control panel," said Serutuf.

Shrad could only scream in anger, fighting to break free, but Sam's grip was strong.

Serutuf disappeared down the opening to the corridor and headed to the ship's main control room.

"How would you like it Shrad, if we brought you back to Earth and kept you there against your will?" said Jamie.

Shrad was silent. He had now abandoned his ranting

and raving.

It took a while for Serutuf to return. When he did, he gave the news that all of Shrad's ship control capabilities were destroyed. He would do no more harm to other peaceful alien vessels. Now they just needed to keep him restrained so they could board their ship and take off.

Before Sam could let go however, a beam of light cut through the air and hit Serutuf square, sending him flying backwards and crashing into the wall.

Janice stood from within the doorway – her eyes glowing red.

"Beautiful! Now put me down and have Erar bring you both back down to size or Janice will reduce all of you to ashes," said Shrad.

"Are you kidding me?" Jamie responded as she proceeded to walk over to Janice and pulverize her with one swing of her fist. Janice broke apart like Steven - her metal innards dancing across the floor.

"No!! I will punish you for that," said Shrad.

"Empty promises, Shrad," said Jamie.

"Serutuf, are you all right?" asked Sam.

I'm fine. The robot caught me by surprise, but my body absorbed the energy. Now we must leave this place. You can release Shrad and board our ship when Erar reduces you again.

After Serutuf boarded the ship, Jamie was reduced to small size again so she could enter the ship. Sam tossed Shrad down the corridor and was also re-sized, quickly boarding the ship.

We are ready for departure, said Erar.

"How do we get out of here? The ship's hatch is

closed," said Sam.

With this, said Serutuf, holding up the familiar orb.
I have transferred the open code from Shrad's computer.

Serutuf placed the orb into a compartment and started pressing a multitude of buttons. The huge ship hatch started to vibrate and slowly open, allowing the crew to fly out of the opening and into the vastness of space.

Chapter Fourteen

Home Again

"Home. We're really going back home," Jamie said with relief.

"Serutuf, what will happen with Shrad? Are you sure he won't come after us again?" said Sam.

Yes. His ship controls are useless now. He has no means of communication as well. He will be left to aimlessly roam the galaxy.

"I like that – trapped in his own ship. The perfect punishment for him," said Jamie.

Sam and Jamie still had lots of questions for Serutuf and Erar, who were more than happy to oblige. The ship continued to speed through space on its journey back to Earth, and it wasn't long before the familiar beautiful blue planet came into view. This site brought enormous joy to Sam and Jamie. They would never take anything on Earth for granted again.

The tiny ship entered Earth's atmosphere and soon found the familiar surroundings of Sam's back yard. Serutuf landed near the trees so as not to be seen.

We only have yet to say our goodbyes and bring you back to your normal size, said Erar.

"We can't thank you guys enough," said Sam.

"I'm very glad to call you my friends," added Jamie.

We are proud to call you our earthly friends, said Erar.

Before you depart, we would like to give you something as our gratitude for what you've done for us. Serutuf held out the shiny metal orb that had done so much to aid in their quest.

"Wow. Really?" said Jamie, accepting the object.

"But when we get larger, it will be too small to see," said Sam.

No. It is programmed to maintain its ratio with whoever is holding it, said Serutuf.

"If you guys are ever in our part of the galaxy again, stop by and say hello," said Sam.

Sam and Jamie endured another enlargement sequence (strangely they were starting to get used to it) and watched as the little spaceship darted off.

"Can you believe everything that just happened?" asked Jamie.

"Not hardly. In any case, it's going to be impossible to explain this to Mom and Gramps," said Sam.

They both stood there soaking up the atmosphere.

"It sure does feel good to be back," said Jamie.

*

Sam, Jamie, Gramps and Mrs. Orzabal all sat around the dining room table. Mrs. Orzabal was emotional and joyful upon seeing them return. But when she was past that and wanted answers.

"I want to know where you two disappeared to for practically a day and a half. Do you know I had the authorities looking for you? I was scared to death!"

"...and don't tell me you were captured by aliens and flew off in a spaceship – you've already convinced Gramps that this is the case."

"But Mom – it's true. You know I wouldn't lie to you about that," said Sam.

"As hard as it is to believe, Aunt Sue, it is true. We wouldn't make up something so ridiculous," said Jamie.

Mrs. Orzabal sighed and shook her head.

"Look – I want to believe you both, but you can understand how that sounds to me."

"I know, Mom," said Sam.

"Do you have any proof that you were part of some alien abduction?" asked Mrs. Orzabal.

Sam and Jamie looked at each other and Jamie reached into her pocket to produce the alien orb.

"Yes," said Jamie.

THE END

www.ingramcontent.com/pod-product-compliance
Lightning Source LLC
Chambersburg PA
CBHW020626130626
46552CB00003B/1103